W9-CAM-048

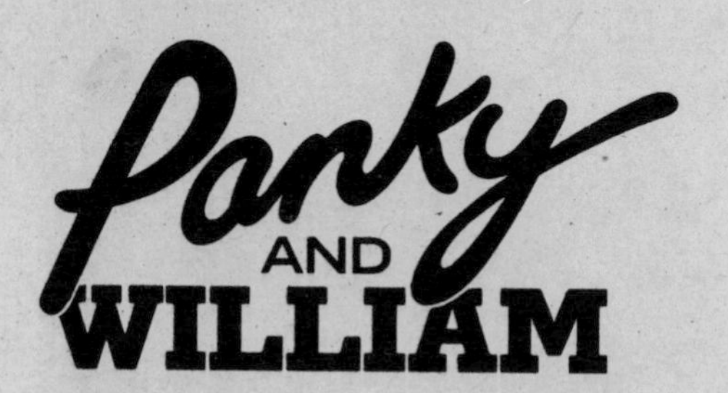
Panky
AND
WILLIAM

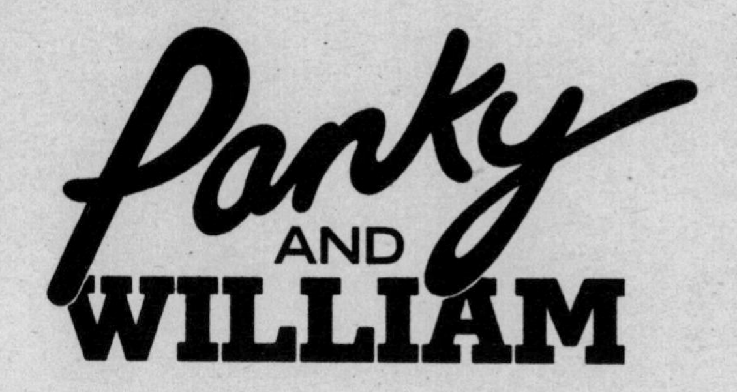

Nancy Saxon

Illustrated by
Charles Saxon

SCHOLASTIC INC.
New York Toronto London Auckland Sydney

ISBN 0-590-33451-4

 Published by Scholastic Inc., 730 Broadway, New York, NY 10003, by arrangement with Atheneum Publishers, Inc.

12 11 10 9 8 7 6 5 4 3 2 5 6 7 8 9/8 0/9

Printed in the U.S.A. 11

To Akiko, with love

CONTENTS

Chapter 1

MOSTLY ABOUT ME

MY NAME IS FRANCES, but nobody calls me that. Usually, I'm called Panky, and Daddy calls me Panky-Poo. I know that's silly, but I like it. Maybe it's the way he says it.

When Mother gets mad, she calls me Frances. Last fall, that was more and more of the time. It's a terrible thing to say, but I used to think Mother didn't like me very much. She was always nagging about something.

It was, "Panky, sit up straight!" or "Panky, hang up your clothes!" or "Frances! Stop eating candy! Do you want to be the fat lady in a circus?"

That last remark really hurt. You see, being fat was my problem. At ten years old,

I was the fattest girl in fifth grade! Maybe I would end up being the fat lady in a circus, but I didn't think my own mother ought to say so!

Sometimes, I dreamed about being in a circus, but I wasn't a fat lady. I was a lion tamer. I wore black boots and carried a long whip that I cracked in the air. Naturally, I never hit anything with it. In fact, the lions were such good friends, they slept with me at night.

Sometimes, I dreamed I was a cowgirl, riding the range on my own horse. I could even see the horse. It was an Appaloosa, one of those spotted horses Indians used to ride. I sauntered along on my Appaloosa and looked at the mountains and the clouds and sang cowboy songs.

I was never fat in my dreams! Even my horse was thin!

Frankly, I don't know when I started being fat. I think I must have gained a lot after we moved here. I was sort of chubby before, but nobody ever called me "Fatty" or "Fatso," the way they did here.

We moved in August, when Daddy got transferred, and it took me a long time to get used to it here. We'd lived before in a town with blocks and sidewalks, the kind of place where you could walk to the store, if you wanted to. Where we live now, all the houses are far apart because the zoning law says you have to have at least one acre of land. Our house is TWO MILES from town, only people here call it "the village." Where we live is called "real country." That means we don't have sidewalks.

This place may be over an hour from the city, but it doesn't feel like real country to me! I think of real country as miles of desert or an African jungle with forests so thick with trees you get lost in them. I wouldn't have minded moving to a place like Africa where I could look at the wild animals!

In September, when I started school, I really got homesick. It seemed to me that what I missed most was sidewalks. Everything I used to do that was fun was on a sidewalk, like playing with roller skates or riding my bicycle. You can't play in the roads here because they're too dangerous.

Another thing I missed was friends! I used to be able to go outside and find somebody to play with. On a summer night, kids on the block would play out, games like hide-and-go-seek and giant steps. I wasn't the leader of the gang or anything, but I was never left out. If you'd asked who my friends were, I'd probably have named everybody in the neighborhood, even people I didn't like much.

The way things were here, it was like being on a desert island. During the day, there was just me and Mother, together on a desert island with a lot of nothing around us. I can tell you one thing about "real country." People in a family can really get on each other's nerves!

Since we were new here, Mother was anxious to do the right thing. Those are her words, not mine. And, believe me, doing the right thing could keep you busy from morning until night. The kids here are into Girl Scouts and swimming lessons at the Y and ballet lessons. I don't know how most of them manage since every place they go is miles from every other place.

Mother settled on one thing for me that she cared about more than all the others. She was dying for me to go to Miss Letitia Finletter's dancing class at the country club. It so happened that, of all the things going on, that was the one I knew I would hate most! You have to wear a party dress and white gloves and patent leather shoes and the boys BOW when they ask you to dance! It's just plain silly! I mean, you see these boys every day at school, and, all of a sudden, you're supposed to act like you're meeting them for the first time! What could be worse!

I knew what I liked, if anybody had asked me. I liked animals! I'd still give anything to have a dog come running to meet me when I get home from school. If it was MY dog, he'd jump up and lick my face and be happy just because it was ME! But I can't have a dog because Mother is allergic to fur.

When I grow up, I'm going to have cats and dogs and horses all over the place. They can sleep on the sofa and sit at the table with me, if they want to. In fact, I think I'd like that!

Chapter 2

SCHOOL

LAST FALL, I thought Monday was the worst day of the week, if any one day was worse than another! All day long, people around me in class were talking and passing notes. I guess they had a lot to talk about after the weekend. If you didn't have a best friend, you might as well be dead as far as having anybody to talk to. And I didn't.

For instance, Tiffany Calder and Jennifer West were best friends, and they both ride on my bus. Tiffany got on first and she always saved a seat for Jennifer. She put books on the seat next to her and nobody would have dreamed of asking her to move them. I knew I wouldn't. When Jennifer got on, she and Tiffany started whispering and giggling. They weren't talking about me.

That is, I don't think they were, but I felt awful just the same. That sort of thing can really put you in a bad humor!

Outside of not having friends, school was OK. Mrs. Mahoney was my teacher, and she was pretty nice. She was young, with short blonde hair, and she wasn't too strict. Most of the time, she let us get up without permission and walk around. We could sharpen pencils and get water and stuff like that. When we were doing something special, like reading or drawing, we had to sit still.

I liked drawing best. My special thing was drawing horses. I've practiced a lot so I'm good at it. Most people draw a horse like a shoebox and put legs at each end. Well, I know horses are very round in the back and a little bit round in front. And the legs don't hang down like spaghetti. They come BEFORE the end of the horse. That one little thing makes a big difference.

One Monday a couple of weeks after school started, I drew this Appaloosa, the one I always dream about, and he was galloping across the prairie with his mane flying in the wind. The desert had a couple of cactus plants, like big green tongues, with pink flowers hanging off them. I colored the sky bright blue and put in a round yellow sun. I didn't draw me because I wasn't that good.

Mrs. Mahoney said, "Why, that's very nice, Panky! May I put it up on the bulletin board?"

Naturally, I said yes.

Katie Riley saw it, and she said, "Panky! That's beautiful! Can I have it?"

I knew Katie was crazy about horses, so I said she could.

Mrs. Mahoney saw us talking. She said, "Katie, would you like to sit in front of Panky?"

"Sure!" said Katie. "I can watch her draw horses!"

Mrs. Mahoney must have noticed that Katie and I were the only ones in class without a special friend. She may even have noticed that I got tired of passing other people's notes!

I decided I was going to like Katie. She was kind of homely, but she was friendly looking. Her hair is red and she wears it in a ponytail. She has lots of freckles, and she grins a lot. Her father is head groom at Fox

Run Hunt Club. Fox Run is fashionable, but Katie, as daughter of the head groom, is not. I don't care about things like that, but I know some people do.

That day, it was Katie's turn to make a two minute talk. Everybody in class had to make a talk about their hobby. I talked about TV shows, since that's all I know anything about. Everybody in class looked at the same shows, so I didn't tell them anything they didn't already know. I'd heard some of the girls singing commercials during recess, and they knew all the words. I don't know why, but I'd be ashamed to sing commercials!

As the time drew near for Katie's talk, I could tell she was getting nervous. She was so still, her ponytail hung down like it was made of stone!

I tapped her on the shoulder.

"Hey," I said. "What's your hobby?"

"Horses," she said, not turning around.

"Real or imaginary?" I said.

The ponytail swung around.

"Real! Of course!" Her face lit up. "I love everything about them. Now that it's getting cold, their coats are all long and shaggy. They feel like teddy bears!"

When I heard that, I felt jealous.

"What's so great about fur?" I said. Actually, I like fur. A lot.

"Are the horses yours?" I went on. I knew they weren't.

Katie grinned.

"No, but they don't know that."

I thought about it. I guess they don't.

I wondered what it would be like to live next to a stable. Pretty nice, I decided.

Mrs. Mahoney introduced Katie, and she walked stiffly to the front of the class. I didn't want to make things worse for her, so I looked out the window. I don't like to stare at people when they're scared.

"Panky," said Mrs. Mahoney. "I think Katie would appreciate it if you paid attention."

I looked at Katie and made a horrible face, showing all my teeth. It's my shark smile, and it's ferocious! Katie giggled, and I did too.

"Now, that's enough," said Mrs. Mahoney.

I didn't care. Katie didn't look so scared anymore.

"My father is head groom at Fox Run Hunt Club," Katie began, "so I have always been associated with horses. I'm lucky because our house is next to the stable and I spend a lot of time over there. I help the grooms with their work."

I had to hand it to her. Most people got up and bragged about how good they were at sailing or tennis and told about the prizes they won at their clubs. It was the same as saying how rich and smart they were.

"I used to think," Katie said, "that horses were just like people, except that they had long faces and four legs."

The class laughed, and Katie turned pink. She must have been pretty young when she thought that!

Katie swallowed hard before starting again.

"In some ways, horses are nicer than people," she said. "They don't criticize you or notice things about you, such as what kind of clothes you wear or how much money you get for an allowance. In other ways, they are hard to figure out. Like once, I was going to give a horse a carrot and I dropped it. When I bent down to pick it up, that horse almost bit my hand off! He thought I wanted to eat the carrot myself! Well, it so happens I hate carrots. But try and tell that to a horse!

"A sick horse is the saddest thing in the world, because he can't tell you what hurts. Sometimes, I think I'd like to be a veterinarian when I grow up so I can help sick animals. But I could never stand to see a horse die. Or any other animal for that matter."

Katie walked back to her desk looking relieved. I thought her talk was very interesting. Katie is a sincere person. If she'd tried to be a big phony, her talk wouldn't have been interesting. I was glad she wanted my picture of the Appaloosa.

I decided to take it down and give it to her at once. People were moving around, the way they always do after they've had to sit still. I wish I'd looked to see who was watching me. That way, I might have known who did it. Because someone had taken a black crayon and drawn a fat girl sitting on the back of my horse. I knew it was supposed to be me, even without my name and an arrow pointing to the girl.

I took the picture down and tore it up. I felt ashamed, and I could feel myself blushing.

"Panky!" said Katie. "What happened?"

I showed her what was left of the picture.

"That's too bad!" said Katie. "I really wanted that picture! I'll bet a boy did it!"

I guess she was right. Anyway, having Katie care made me feel a little better, but not a whole lot. Mondays are always lousy!

The ride home on the bus wasn't much fun either. Tiffany and Jennifer giggled all the way. Honestly, I think they ought to move in with each other!

The first thing I did when I got home was go to the kitchen for a snack. Mother called from upstairs.

"Is that you, Panky?"

I came out in the hall and said it was.

"Don't spoil your appetite," she said. "We're having a nice supper."

"OK," I said.

I went back in the kitchen and made myself a peanut butter sandwich. Then I had a couple of brownies for dessert. That should have been enough, but I was still hungry. I looked around for something else and found a chicken casserole in the refrigerator. I must have eaten half of it when I heard Mother.

"Panky! That was supposed to be supper!"

Mother was staring at what was left of the casserole. Then she got mad.

"That does it!" she said. "You're going on a diet, starting tomorrow!"

And I had thought things were as bad as they could get. Believe me! They got worse!

Chapter 3

THE DIET

TUESDAY WAS the first day of the diet. I came home from school hungrier than usual because Mother had packed me a diet lunch. I ran to the kitchen and tore open the door to the refrigerator. Well, that refrigerator was so empty, it was like seeing it for the first time. There was a light bulb I didn't know was there and a lot of empty wire shelves. The only food was a bowl of carrots, cut into little sticks. Mother had planted a note in them: EAT ME. Very funny! I tried to eat them, but it was like chewing dead twigs. I spit them into the garbage and started looking for the usual brownies or cakes. There weren't any! I told myself I wanted to lose weight and I ought to be glad, but I wasn't.

I tried to take my mind off food by looking at television. That didn't work. In case you haven't noticed, a lot of commercials are about food. It's just awful, when you're hungry, to look at commercials for fried chicken or cake mix or potato chips! You can even hear them chewing the potato chips! Actually, if I think about it in time, I don't have to *listen*. Daddy put something called a "blab-off" on our set. All you have to do is press this little button, and the sound goes off. But, even without sound, it's torture to watch people eating the very things you aren't supposed to have!

At five-thirty, Mother called me in to my so-called dinner. She put a plate in front of me and stood nearby, sipping sherry and pretending not to notice. Dinner was celery and fish cooked in water. It's the first time I'd seen fish cooked any way but fried. It was all limp and dead and there wasn't any crust. I can't imagine who eats it that way, unless they have to. I ate it because I was starving. Anyway, with Mother watching, I didn't have a choice.

About an hour later, Mother pulled the good food out from wherever she had hidden it and cooked supper for Daddy. The whole house began to smell of onions, pot roast, and fried potatoes! Smells can really drive you crazy!

Daddy got home from the city at seven. He gave me a big hug and said, "How's my girl?" but he didn't want a big discussion. It's sort of understood that I'm supposed to look at television and let Mother and Daddy talk. Daddy always has a martini while Mother tells him everything that went wrong that day. This usually involves plumbing or gutters or stuff like that.

That night, Mother said, "What did you have for lunch today?"

And Daddy said, "Pot roast."

Mother said, "That's too bad because I've got pot roast for supper. What did you have for dessert?"

Daddy said, "Chocolate mousse."

Mother said, "Oh, another one of those expense account lunches. What did you drink?"

Daddy said, "One Bloody Mary," emphasizing the one.

I certainly hoped they didn't keep this up. There must be something to talk about besides food!

I went upstairs thinking of all the things I wanted to eat and couldn't. I read a horse book until late, but I don't know how I ever fell asleep.

For the next few days, I ate nothing but tasteless food, and I was hungry all the time! Then, I felt myself getting crafty and greedy. I'd do anything to get something good to eat! My first chance came when I went to the supermarket with Mother. Without meaning to, I found myself standing right by the candy rack! It only took a minute to pick up two Snickers and a Hershey bar and pay for them in the fast check-out line. Mother didn't even notice!

Maybe, I should have felt guilty, but I didn't!

After that, I bought candy whenever I could and sneaked it into my room. I had chocolate chip cookies in the backs of drawers and stuffed cake in my shoebag. I even put a Hershey bar under my pillow. The electric blanket must have gotten to that because it melted and stuck to the pillow case.

At the end of two weeks, I'd gained five pounds!

Mother was wild! I heard her telling Daddy about it. They didn't think I was listening because I was watching TV.

"I'm at my wit's end," said Mother. "Panky is absolutely gross! You'd think she would want to look pretty. Somewhere I must have failed. I should have started sooner with the yogurt and cottage cheese.

Daddy said something to the effect that things weren't all that bad.

"You haven't seen her room lately," said Mother. "It's so full of crumbs, we're getting mice. Sometimes," she added, "I think she eats just to spite me!"

I held my breath to hear what Daddy would say.

"She always looks cute to me," he said.

I didn't know why, but I felt like crying. I knew I wasn't likable. The way I was, I didn't even like myself!

Later that evening, when Mother and

Daddy were watching an old movie, I slipped down to the kitchen. There was a half a lemon pie Mother had forgotten to hide. I ate it all! I even licked the plate!

Chapter 4

REAL HORSES

I DREW ANOTHER horse for Katie. I didn't feel like it, after what happened to my other picture, so I waited a long time to do it. But one day I did. I wanted Katie to like me.

Katie said not to make this one an Appaloosa because they didn't have those at Fox Run.

I was curious.

"What do you have?" I asked.

"Lots of different breeds," said Katie. "We have Thoroughbreds and quarter horses and a few Arabians. You'll love drawing Arabians! They look like something out of a fairy tale. They have thin noses and beautiful eyes with long eyelashes. You could draw them with wings or a little horn. You could make one into a unicorn!"

So I drew a unicorn standing in a green field with yellow flowers springing up around him. Katie loved it!

Then I had an idea.

"I wish I could see horses up close," I said. "I know I could draw them better if I could see them right in front of me."

"That's a good idea!" said Katie. "How about coming home with me today? Of course," she added, "I have chores to do."

"I'll help you with them," I said. Katie couldn't know how much it meant to me to go home with her. Part of it was that I needed a friend. But besides that, I was thrilled to think I might get to see real horses.

Katie agreed, but she warned me. "Cleaning out a stall takes practice. My father says anybody can learn to ride, but good grooms are made in heaven."

I laughed. Nothing could have discouraged me! I had been dreaming about horses for a long time.

I rode home on the bus with Katie. I'm

not sure I'm supposed to, but the driver didn't seem to notice.

Katie lived in a tiny house only a few yards from the stable. It looked the way I picture the witch's cottage in Hansel and Gretel. Katie's mother was anything but an old witch. To me, that day, she smelled as if she were made of cookies. As a matter of fact, she had just been baking, and she offered us some chocolate chip cookies. All Katie wanted was a bunch of carrots for the horses, so I was ashamed to eat more than one.

"Panky's a horse artist," said Katie. "And we're going over to the stables."

We raced next door.

I liked the smell of the stable. It was a real country smell. At least, it smelled like real country to me. It smelled of hay and polished leather and horses! A groom was sweeping the concrete aisle, kicking dust motes up into the sunlight. I noticed a swallow building a nest in the rafters. And, best of all, there were horses on either side of the aisle, dozens of them! They knew Katie and they hung their heads over their stall gates, whinnying impatiently. Katie broke the carrots into little pieces and gave one to each horse.

"My father says this is 'cupboard love'," she said, "but I don't care. They really do like me!"

Katie showed me how to hold out my hand and let the horse nibble off of it.

"There's a reason for everything with horses," she said. "If you stick your fingers out when you feed them, you might get bitten. My father's missing one finger and that's how it happened.

If she'd told me that before, I might not have been so brave! Katie walked down the aisle, introducing me to the horses.

She said, "Boris, this is Panky. She's my best friend."

Boris sort of rolled his eyes around funny and stared down his nose at me. I thought he might be trying to make up his mind to bite me; but Katie said not to worry, Boris was the safest horse in the stable. Besides, he would know I was all right because I was with her.

I said, "Hello, Boris."

I met all the horses on that aisle.

"Hello, Boris! Hello, Lightfoot! Hello, Carrot Top! Hello, Dixie! Hello, Cupcake! Hello, Rocket! Hello, Duffy! Hello, Bye-Bye! Hello, Sweet Pea!"

Then we got to work, cleaning out the stalls. Katie was a hard worker, and she taught me a lot. I did my best to be a real help.

After we had cleaned three stalls, Katie said, "Well! Have you learned anything?"

I'd never known horses were so much work! It was unbelievable! But I didn't want to complain.

"I mean about drawing them," said Katie.

I stepped back and looked at a horse. They're so big, you don't see what they're like close up; at least, not to draw. I noticed something I'd never seen before. Horses have big feet! I'd been drawing little stumps, but the foot is shaped like a bell that's swinging out in front!

"I never noticed what big feet they have!" I said.

"That's right," said Katie. "I'm glad you drew my unicorn standing in the grass."

The hours passed quickly, and soon it was time for Katie to go and help her mother and for me to go home. Katie invited me to come back. She said when the horses got used to me, I could help groom them. I could hardly wait!

It was a long walk home, but I didn't mind.

Mother was waiting for me at the door, and she looked cross.

"Where on earth have you been?" she said. "Do you realize that it's five o'clock?"

"I went home with Katie," I said. "I've been helping her clean out stalls!" I was kind of proud of it.

Mother looked furious. "You've been working in a stable?" she said. "And I can't get you to hang up your clothes at home!"

I didn't see any reason for her to get mad!

She didn't say anymore, but I could tell she was thinking. I figured she was thinking she wanted me to be friends with what she called the "better class families." In this town, people are divided into "commuters" and "townies," and the commuters think they're better. Don't ask me why. I think people ought to be just people. My mother isn't really mean, but we were new here and she didn't want to make mistakes. Working in a stable wasn't her idea of how to get ahead socially!

We both thought our own private thoughts for a day or two. What I thought was that I wanted Katie for a friend and that I would go to the stables whenever I had a chance. What with that and sneaking food, I felt as if I were practically a criminal type!

Mother must have decided that I needed friends and it was up to her to help me get them. So, one morning, without even asking me, she called Jennifer's mother and invited Jennifer over to play.

I wish somebody had told Mother she couldn't make friends for me. It was embarrassing! Anyway, Jennifer couldn't come.

"Jennifer has lessons every afternoon after school," Mother explained.

I could have told her that. Most of the kids in my class have some kind of lesson every afternoon.

"She has a tennis lesson today," said Mother, "but you're invited to go along."

I had the feeling Mother had accepted, and I was right.

I didn't want to go, the most important reason being that my jeans didn't fit anymore. I could only get the zipper halfway up, and then I had to fold the little tab over and hope it stayed.

"Wear your jeans," said Mother. "Jennifer's mother will pick you all up after school and I'll bring you home."

"I can't go," I said. "My jeans don't fit."

Mother didn't care.

"It won't matter for one day," she said. "If you like tennis, I'll buy you a jogging suit. Jennifer's mother says they play in jogging suits when it's cold."

I gave up. It would be embarrassing to back out. I wished Mother had asked me first. I wasn't sure Jennifer liked me! In fact, I didn't think she did.

Anyway, at two thirty, I found myself waiting with Jennifer and Tiffany and another girl in our class, Tara Winslow. Tiffany and Jennifer wore jogging suits and matching hair ribbons. Tara had on a tennis dress with a sweater over it.

"Why didn't you tell me what you were wearing!" said Tara. "I'd have worn *my* jogging suit!"

That's just like Tara. She worries a lot about what people think of her. She's the kind of person who'll tear off the plastic squares on a Rubik cube and stick them back on right and say SHE did it. I know, because I saw her do it!

She wants to be like Tiffany and Jennifer, but they're always ahead of her. They try to be! They used to wear jeans until everybody started wearing them. Then, they started wearing overalls, like they're old farmers, or something.

When you're fat, you can't worry about that sort of thing. I was wearing my jeans with the zipper halfway up. I used a big safety pin to hold the sides together. The pin was bent and I was afraid it was going to pop loose any minute. I had left my shirt out all day to cover everything up.

If I got any fatter, I would have to start wearing dresses. That would be too bad, because in our school, we do a lot of sitting on the floor and the floor's pretty dirty! Besides, nobody wears dresses to school. I didn't want to be *that* different.

Well, Jennifer's mother came by in her station wagon and took us to the racquet club. When we got out of the car, it was like somebody pushed a button. Everybody went wild, running toward the courts and screaming. I walked slowly to our court. I was worried about the safety pin. Besides I didn't see any point in running.

It's a funny thing. I've watched kids in carpools and I always got the feeling they were all good friends and having fun together. Well, here I was in a carpool and I wasn't having any fun. I guess people don't have to like each other just because they're in the same carpool.

The racquet club was cold because it

was too big to heat. There was a curving roof, like a big tent, and a row of tennis courts. Most of the courts were filled with grown people, swatting the ball back and forth as if they were having a war. Our instructor was wearing white shorts and a shirt with Kevin written on it.

Kevin asked my name, and I told him.

"Panky", he said, "you must grip your racket as if you were shaking hands with it. And remember to turn to the side when you swing at the ball. You'll soon catch up with the others."

He took turns hitting the ball to each of us. I missed when it was my turn.

Then we played something called "hot potato." We were supposed to keep the ball going back and forth across the net for as long as we could without missing it! It was awful! There were six of us on each side, and everybody was swinging HARD, as if they didn't care who was in the way. I had to do a lot of running to keep from getting hit. You can guess what happened! All of a sudden, the safety pin stabbed me, and I let out a yell! There was so much noise, nobody noticed until I started limping away.

"Did you turn your ankle?" said Kevin.

"Yes," I lied.

"Better take it easy," he said.

I sat out the rest of the lesson.

Mother picked us up. The other girls had brought along money for the Coke machine, but Mother wouldn't let me have one because of the calories. All the way home, the rest of them were sipping their drinks with straws and rattling the ice.

"Isn't tennis great?" said Jennifer.

I thought it was terrible, but I didn't say so. By that time, I felt like some kind of freak!

Chapter 5

I GET A NICKNAME

THREE WEEKS had gone by since I started the diet. Mother gave me less and less to eat and I ate more and more in my room. I knew I had to do something to take my mind off food. If I could have spent more time at Fox Run, it would have been different, but I knew Mother wouldn't like that.

Finally, I came up with the idea of taking my stickers to school. I've been collecting a long time and I must have about a million. I thought if I took them to school, I'd be so busy showing them off, I wouldn't have time to be hungry. It would work for one day, at least. After that, I'd think of something else.

I'd have to be careful with them. Things get lost at school. Once I had brought a giant rubber pencil, about two feet long, that you could twist around like a pretzel. It disappeared, and the next thing I knew Scott Morrison had it on his desk and he wouldn't give it back. He said he had found it!

The little kids bring Snoopy dolls and teddy bears to school and nothing ever happens to them. They'd yell their heads off if it did!

I carried my album of stickers in a shopping bag. It weighed about a ton, but I managed to get on the bus with it. When I got to school, it was just the way I thought it would be. Everybody crowded around, looking, asking where I had gotten a certain sticker. I felt pretty good! Then, Mrs. Mahoney said, "Panky, we have work to do. How about showing your stickers during lunch hour?"

That was OK with me. I thought I might even forget to eat. If I knew Mother, my lunch wasn't worth eating anyway.

When I opened my album in the cafeteria, everybody started coming over.

Tiffany saw a sticker she wanted, and she said, "How about trading me for this one?"

It was a googley-eyed rabbit, one of my favorites.

I said, "What for?"

She didn't have any stickers with her.

Tiffany thought for a while.

"Dessert?" she said.

I looked at her tray. Dessert was chocolate cake, something I happen to like better than anything in the world.

"OK" I said, pulling out the rabbit and handing it to her.

Then Jennifer wanted to swap her dessert for a sticker.

Tara saw what was happening and she came over with a half-eaten dish of ice cream.

"How about trading with me?" she said. "I only took one bite."

I could see she'd eaten more than that, but I didn't know how to say no.

Joey Watson came by. He took one look at me with all those desserts and yelled out, "Panky Pig! Panky Pig! What are you eating? Corn?"

I could have gone right through the floor! The girls sort of drifted away then. I guess they didn't want to be associated with me. There I sat, alone with my stickers, two pieces of cake, and a dish of melting ice cream.

I heard the chair next to me scrape, and Katie sat down.

"I heard that, Panky," she said. "It was really mean!"

I felt a tear roll down my face.

"They hate me!" I said.

"I don't hate you," said Katie. "I like you. I liked you right away. You're the only one who ever wanted to come home with me."

I could tell she meant it. I don't think Katie would say anything she didn't mean.

"Let's eat," said Katie. "We're not going to let any old boy make us feel bad!"

She opened her lunch pail. It was an ugly, gun-metal gray, the kind of pail work-men use. But wonderful smells came out of it! Katie unwrapped two tiny, biscuit sandwiches, filled with ham and swiss cheese. It made my mouth water to look at them. Then, she took out deviled eggs, a container of chocolate pudding, and oatmeal cookies.

"My mother's a great cook," said Katie, "but she gives me too much. Here! Have some."

I took a biscuit sandwich and ate it in two bites. I ended up eating the chocolate pudding, too. Somehow, I couldn't eat the desserts I traded for. It made me feel bad to look at them!

The lunch Mother had packed was a stalk of celery with the leaves still on it, and a soggy cucumber sandwich. I gave Katie the celery.

"I'll tell you what," said Katie. "Why don't you come over again next week? It was really neat having you help me! That is, if you didn't mind!"

That made me feel a little better. Of course, I didn't mind helping Katie! I loved it! I didn't care what my mother thought. I wanted to go home with Katie, and I would!

I managed to get through the rest of the time at school, but I felt really bad. "Panky Pig!" Everybody in school would hear my new nickname before the day was over. If only I had said something back, something to show I didn't care. But I did care! And I couldn't think of anything smart to say, even now. What I felt like doing was throwing things!

I wished I could go home with Katie, but she hadn't invited me for today.

Chapter 6

THE TANTRUM

MY BRIGHT IDEA of taking stickers to school had backfired. I felt lousy all afternoon. Who wouldn't with a nickname like mine! Just before supper, I went to my room and ate two Snickers. I ate them so fast, I hardly tasted them. I was starting on stale pound cake when Mother called. I stuffed the cake in a sock.

Supper was spinach and liver, two things I despise. I pushed my plate back and howled.

"I want fried chicken! I want chocolate cake! I want candy!"

Mother turned pale.

"Panky, dear," she said weakly, "we don't keep sweets in the house. You know that."

"Yes, you do!" I shouted. "There's a pumpkin pie in the freezer, and I want it right now!"

Mother had never seen me like that before. I don't usually get mad; or, if I do, I don't show it.

"Well, I suppose one little slice wouldn't hurt," she said.

She got the pie out of the freezer and put it in the oven.

"I want it now!" I yelled.

Mother hurriedly dropped the pie in front of me. I guess she thought I'd be ashamed to eat a whole pie, but I wasn't. I ate every bite, ice slivers and all!

I felt kind of sick when I got through, but I wasn't sorry.

Mother looked unhappy.

"I don't see how you'll ever get to dancing class," she said. "And I had so wanted to buy you a pretty dress! Now you're even popping out of your jeans!"

She appeared to suddenly make up her mind about something. She went to the pantry and pulled down a white box.

"Panky, I do want to help," she said. "Here's a little something I picked up for you in the Village."

She tried to smile. It was a thin, quavery smile. It made me think of a flapping sheet held to the clothesline by a single pin. I almost felt sorry for her.

I opened the box. Under layers of tissue paper, there was something white and lacy.

"It's a panty girdle," Mother explained.

I hurled the box and its contents in Mother's direction and ran towards the stairs.

"I hate you!" I shouted.

I slammed the door to my room and locked it. I yanked out drawers and emptied them on the floor. Food and clothes tumbled out. I swept my collection of glass animals off the shelf and watched them break in little pieces. What good were glass animals? I'd rather have nothing!

Then I threw myself on the bed and cried.

When Daddy got home, there was no supper waiting for him. He came up to my room and made me open the door. His

mouth fell open with astonishment when he saw the mess. Then he quietly got a dustpan and a broom and cleaned up. He didn't try to talk, and I was glad. When he had finished, he carried the dustpan, filled with tiny glass slivers, down to the kitchen.

Mother was there weeping.

"She was such a beautiful baby!" she sobbed. "When she was born, the nurse brought her in and she had one little black curl with a pink bow tied on it. I thought she was the sweetest thing I'd ever seen! And remember how she looked in her little Easter dress when she was four? It was blue organdy with a starched white pinafore. I can still remember the way she looked, hunting for Easter eggs!"

It was all in the past tense. I might as well be dead.

"Now, she hates me!" Mother's voice broke. "Sometimes, I think a wicked fairy took away my beautiful baby and left Panky in her place!"

"She doesn't hate you," said Daddy. "Someday, she'll appreciate what you're trying to do for her."

"Panky's never cared for the things I like," said Mother.

"She's herself," said Daddy. "She has to find out what SHE likes. We have to let her find out."

This met with silence.

"It's not that you're wrong," said Daddy. "But it's not enough to TELL people what they ought to be. Most of us need bridges."

For the first time, I felt that someone might understand. I remembered the time at camp when I got pushed off the high diving board. I looked at the water all the way down and almost smacked my eyes out! I never went out on the diving board again. That's how I felt now with Mother pushing me to do things I didn't want to do!

"I've had all I can take for one day," said Mother, coldly. "Panky will come down when she's hungry."

That was pretty sarcastic talk from someone who had just been weeping about fairies and lost babies. Well, I'd show her! I wouldn't come down if I starved to death!

Chapter 7

A SPECIAL KIND OF DOCTOR

I DREAMED I was helping Katie groom horses and it was wonderful! The horses really liked me! You could tell. When I came down the aisle, they stomped and nickered, just the way they did for Katie.

Then I woke up. It was morning, and Mother was talking in her loudest voice.

"She's still gaining!" she said. "I don't know where she gets candy and cake, but she does! I'm at the end of my rope!"

Daddy said something about "growing pains" and fat not being the only thing that mattered.

Mother had something on her mind.

"It's time to get professional help," she said.

I wondered what she meant. I didn't like the sound of it.

After Daddy left to catch his train, Mother made several telephone calls. I know one of them was to Mrs. Mahoney because I heard her name. It sounded like I wouldn't be going to school. The only way I could find out what was going on was to go downstairs. So I did.

Mother explained in a nervous, hurried way.

"We're going to see a special kind of doctor, Panky. He's called a psychiatrist."

It sounded worse than dentist!

Mother wasn't interested in breakfast. With no supper the night before, except, of course, the pumpkin pie, it had been a long time since I had eaten. I was ravenous! I fixed myself a small mountain of sugarless cereal and poured skimmed milk over it.

After eating, I dressed, and Mother drove us to the psychiatrist's office.

She went in first while I sat in the waiting room. It was a long wait, long enough for me to get good and scared. By the time I was summoned, I was plenty nervous.

What's more, I didn't like the looks of the doctor. I was used to nice old Dr. Miller in his wrinkled white coat. He always gave me a big hug and told me how much I'd grown. This doctor was young, and he wore a plain business suit. I guess psychiatrists don't worry about germs.

"Ah, young lady!" He waved me to a chair. "Do be seated."

There was a big leather chair facing his desk. I managed to bump into it as I sat down.

"Instant gratification. I think that's the problem we are dealing with."

He said it like he was talking to a roomful of people.

"We want WHAT we want WHEN we want it."

I sank back into the chair. I didn't think I was going to like this.

"If we eat too much, we gain weight. Am I correct?"

I said yes.

"We want to change that, Panky."

He smiled, trying to be friendly. That almost made it worse.

"If you'll stick to Mother's diet, Panky, you'll soon be normal."

Instead of something out of a zoo! I thought. The way he put things was really terrible!

"I understand that at school you are called 'Panky Pig'."

I wanted to sink right through the floor. So Mother knew about my nickname. Mrs. Mahoney must have told her.

"It will take a lot of will power," said the doctor, "but you can do it. You don't have to be 'Panky Pig.' Think how proud you'll be when you lose weight! I imagine Mother has a present in mind for you, sort of a reward."

He looked expectantly at Mother.

"She can have patent leather shoes and white gloves and a new dress, and she can go to Miss Finletter's dancing class at the country club!" Mother said it all in one breath. "I can just see Panky, whirling happily around the dance floor in a yellow organdy dress!"

She was positively starry-eyed.

That was the worst moment of my life! It was easier to imagine myself as Captain

Ahab chasing Moby Dick than dressed up in a yellow party dress! And the rest of it was awful! White gloves! Patent leather shoes!

When we got home, I went to my room and ate so much I threw up. They might as well flatten me out like dough and cut out a new Panky! If only someone would say, "What do YOU think Panky?" or "What would YOU like, Panky?"

Mother told Daddy about it that night. I blabbed off the TV and heard every word.

"She's going to get a new dress as a reward; but, first, she has to lose a lot of weight."

"Are you sure a dress is what Panky wants?" said Daddy. He sounded tired.

"It's what she SHOULD want," said Mother. "What Panky wants is to eat herself into a stupor."

That night, I dreamed I was being dragged, kicking and screaming, into the psychiatrist's office. There, I was forced into a hideous yellow dress so tight I could hardly breathe!

Chapter 8

SOMEONE WORSE OFF THAN ME

I TOLD KATIE about the psychiatrist the next day over lunch.

"At first," I said, "he looked at me so hard, I felt like a bug under a microscope. Then, he started talking about how fat I was. He said if I lost weight, I'd get a reward. Mother suggested a yellow dress. She's dying to send me to dancing class, and she can't understand why I don't just love the idea!"

Katie listened sympathetically.

"Personally," she said, "I can't picture you in a yellow dress."

"Neither can I!" I said.

Katie noticed me hungrily eyeing her lunch.

"Oh, that," she said. "Help yourself."

I ate most of Katie's lunch, which was macaroni pie. I left one little bite, without the cheese.

Katie looked at it in a critical way.

"Are you always so hungry?" she said.

I had to admit that I was. Katie wouldn't understand, but I always wanted to eat the whole pie or the whole cake or whatever it was I saw! I felt suddenly ashamed. I quickly offered Katie a low-fat yogurt. I wanted to explain but I couldn't. The truth was, I was never full, no matter how much I ate. It was really weird! I could feel myself getting fatter and uglier with every mouthful, but I couldn't stop!

"I know someone worse off than you," said Katie. "He kicks and bites!"

I hadn't started kicking and biting yet, but there were times when I felt like it.

"He acts like he hates the whole world," said Katie.

"He must be gross!" I said. "How much does he weigh?"

"Several hundred pounds," said Katie,

"but that's not his problem. Come over to Fox Run and look in the third stall from the door."

She was talking about a horse. I should have known!

"We've only had him a few days and he may not stay," said Katie. "He even bites other horses!"

I laughed.

"Hey, why not come home with me today?" said Katie. "You can see him for yourself."

"Sure!" I said. I didn't care what Mother thought.

I went home with Katie on her bus. While she was putting her things away, I found the third stall from the door. The gate was posted with signs:

NO OATS. DO NOT PET. VICIOUS ANIMAL.

A small black horse put his head over the gate and stared at me. Tangled black hair hung over eyes as smoky and deep as pools. They were sad eyes, wistful and frightened. My heart went out to him. I noticed a straw caught in his mane, and I reached out to take it away.

"Watch out, little girl!" a groom snapped. "He'll take your hand off!"

I snatched my hand back.

"What's his name?" I said, pretending not to be nervous.

"He doesn't have one," said the groom, "but I can think of several. If he doesn't stop misbehaving, he's going to end up in a can of dog food."

It took a moment for the horror of this to sink in.

"You mean he might be put to death?"

The boy grinned and went on with his sweeping.

No wonder the little horse was sad! No one loved him, and a truly awful fate might lie ahead. He had probably come from the West, Wyoming or Montana, where he had freely roamed the range. I could picture him racing with other stallions, his nostrils flared, snorting his independence!

I looked around me. The groom had disappeared. I put my hands behind my back, to be on the safe side, and sang:

"Oh, give me a home,
Where the buffalo roam
Where the deer and the antelope play,
Where seldom is heard,
A discouraging word,
And the skies are not cloudy all day."

The little horse never took his sad, liquid eyes off mine. I couldn't believe that he wanted to bite me! I took a chance and stroked his soft nose.

He whinnied, and I almost fell over backwards! I bumped into a gray-haired man in riding breeches. He smiled down at me, his eyes twinkling.

"So you like horses?" he said.

"I like this one," I answered.

"He's a challenge," said the man. "A real horsewoman might make something out of him. By the way," he extended his hand, "I'm Hugo, the riding instructor here. I'm on my way to give a lesson now. Would you care to watch?"

"Yes!" I said.

I followed him outside to a riding ring where about five girls were waiting on their

horses. Hugo walked to the center of the ring and put his hands on his hips.

I climbed up on the rail fence to watch.

"Good afternoon, ladies!" he said, "Let's get right to work! It's too cold to stand around. We'll let Carrot Top take the lead."

Carrot Top was really cute! He was almost as cute as the poor little horse in the third stall. He was sort of red-colored, and he had white socks and a blaze of white down his nose.

"Caroline!" said Hugo. "Don't ask your

horse to go, and then pull back on the reins! Mindy! Your reins are hanging like a clothes-line. Get him on the bit or he'll stumble."

I hardly noticed when Katie climbed up beside me.

The horses picked up speed, and the girls began to go up and down.

"They're posting," said Katie.

I was too absorbed to talk. The lesson lasted one hour, and Katie sat and watched with me. When it was over, Katie climbed down from the fence.

"I'm glad you came home with me, Panky," she said, "but I've got to help Mother now."

She started for her house.

"Katie!" I ran to catch up with her.

"The little horse is marvelous! I don't think he's mean. He has the saddest eyes I ever saw, and his mane is beautiful! That is, it would be, if anyone brushed it. His bangs hang down in his eyes."

"Forelock," Katie corrected. "I agree with you, Panky. That horse could use some help."

"I wish I could take care of him," I said.

Katie nodded. "He needs someone like you, Panky!"

I knew one thing. I'd rather take care of that horse than go to see a psychiatrist!

"I'll come back tomorrow," I said. "That is, if it's all right with you. I sure hope I don't have to go see that doctor!

"I don't care for doctors either," said Katie. "There's a sign on William's gate, put there, no doubt, by some well meaning doctor: NO OATS. If William could only talk! I know he wants all the oats he can get! Don't tell anybody, but I'm sneaking oats to him at night."

William! So that was his name! It suited him. It was a serious, thoughtful name. It was definitely not the name of an animal that might get turned into dog food!

"I don't know what makes him so wild," said Katie. "Spurs and the lash of a crop, no doubt. William wouldn't stand for that!"

I was thinking of what Katie had said about oats.

"Katie!" I said. "Does the doctor think

William would be different if he stopped eating oats?"

"That the general idea!" said Katie.

I knew that couldn't be true. William needed a friend, someone who cared about him. Katie was nice to all the horses, but she didn't have nearly enough time for him. How I wished I could help. William needed all the attention he could get.

"I'm so glad you're sneaking him oats!" I said, feeling grateful.

Chapter 9

ANOTHER VISIT TO THE DOCTOR

PICTURE A ROUND wad of tuna fish, right out of the can, sitting in a puddle of water on a sick-looking lettuce leaf! Mother must have a low opinion of me to give me such a disgusting supper! I mean, that stuff was garbage!

After eating it, I had to listen to her complain about me to Daddy. I was still too fat! I was late coming home! I didn't try to make friends! I didn't have to listen, but I guess I like to torture myself.

"It all falls on me!" said Mother. "You're in the city all day. I'm the one who sits home and begs her to eat cottage cheese!"

"What do you expect me to do?" said

Daddy. "I have to make a living. I can't sit home all day and hold your hand."

There was an angry silence.

"I'm going back to that doctor," said Mother. "He's the only one I can turn to."

"Everything you think of costs money," said Daddy. "It's YOUR job to teach Panky to be a young lady, not a doctor's."

Daddy was finally answering back, but I wasn't sure I liked it.

I covered up my ears and tried to think about horses. I imagined I was at Fox Run, walking down the aisle, like Katie, patting each horse and speaking to him. I said their names out loud.

"Hello, Boris, Dusty, Carrot Top, Lightfoot, Sweet Pea."

I did it again after I went to bed and fell asleep still saying their names. It was like counting sheep.

The next day, Mother picked me up at school. She said we were going to drop by the doctor's, to talk a bit more about "our" problems.

When we got there, Mother went in first. I could hear everything she said, if I listened hard.

"Nobody appreciates me," she began. "Panky hardly speaks to me, and her father's away all day. It's easy for him." Her voice grew bitter. "He has a secretary wait on him hand and foot. He eats big, fancy lunches on the company expense account. I have to stay home and clean out toilet bowls! I don't even have a cleaning woman!"

She paused, I suppose, to catch her breath.

"I try to BE there when Panky comes home from school, but sometimes she's late, and when she does come, she doesn't even say hello. She just rushes past me to get to the refrigerator. That is, she used to go to the refrigerator. Now, she goes to her room. I think she's hiding food there!"

I imagined the doctor was trying to look sympathetic.

"I wish HE had to stay home and watch Panky, and I could go to a fancy office with a secretary!"

I couldn't figure out who made Mother angrier, Daddy or me.

When the hour was almost up, the doctor said, "Well, shall we call in the patient?"

I took the seat facing the doctor. He was still anxiously watching Mother.

"Ah, men shall work and women weep. 'Twas ever so!"

I had considered asking his opinion about William and this mysterious oats business. Now, I put the idea right out of my mind.

Frowning, the doctor turned to me.

"Mother says you don't speak to her when you come home from school. Is that true, Panky?"

There was no point denying it with Mother right there.

"I guess so," I mumbled.

"She's gained five pounds in one week!" said Mother. "She's not gaining on what I feed her."

I should say I wasn't!

"She needs will power," said the doctor,

falling into Mother's habit of speaking of me as if I weren't there.

"Panky, are you trying to make your mother unhappy?"

"No," I said.

I wasn't trying to make Mother anything. All I wanted was to be left alone.

The doctor wasn't finished.

"Who do you think does the marketing? Cooks your food? Washes your clothes? Does the mending?"

He glanced at Mother to see if he had left anything out.

"From now on, Panky, speak to your mother when you come home from school. Ask her if she's had a nice day. Offer to help with the chores."

I thought this was the worst advice I'd ever heard. Mother already nagged me plenty about keeping my room neat, and I didn't like it one bit!

"Panky, why do you eat so much?"

The question took me by surprise.

"I don't have anybody to talk to," I

heard myself say. "I have Katie at school, but, when I get home, there's nobody."

The doctor decided, for reasons of his own, that the visit was over. He stood up rather quickly.

"We'll go into this next week," he said.

I felt really beaten down, but Mother didn't feel that way. On the way home, she was almost in a good humor.

"I have every confidence in your doctor, Panky. I think his grasp of the problem is remarkable!"

I certainly didn't think so! I wished Mother would go to see him without me. She got more out of the visits than I did. Personally, I'd rather be cleaning out stalls!

Chapter 10

GROOMING WILLIAM

I KNEW there would be a big argument if I told Mother I was going to Fox Run, so I went without telling her. I tried to get over as often as I could to help Katie. When Mother asked where I'd been, I would say, "Oh, playing with friends."

That wasn't exactly a lie. The horses *were* my friends, especially William. And I think Mother was so disgusted at me by that time, she was glad not to have me around, reminding her of how fat I was and how her diet wasn't working.

What I actually did was work, and work hard, cleaning out stalls. Katie was nice about it, but she wanted things done exactly right. In the beginning, I followed her around and tried to do everything the way she did. After a while, Katie trusted me to clean out a stall on my own. She led the horse outside and fastened him to a ring on the wall, leaving the stall empty for me to clean.

The first thing I did was scoop up manure with a shovel and take it to a pile outside the stable. There was a layer of leaves and a layer of manure, and together they made fertilizer for gardens. Then I took out wet straw with a pitchfork, being careful not to take dry straw along with it. Then I brought in fresh straw and spread it around so the concrete floor wouldn't hurt the horse's feet. The last thing I did was scrub out the watering pail and bring in fresh water.

It was dirty work, but I didn't mind. While I did it, I was getting to know the horses. I will admit, I was surprised that horses were so much work! I used to think they stood around in fields and ate grass! The truth is, they're big babies! You have to do everything for them, except eat. They're good at that!

After a couple of weeks of cleaning stalls, Katie showed me how to groom a horse. I started on Boris because he's the quietest horse in the stable. As soon as I learned how, Katie let me groom William.

Honestly, I don't think anybody did a thing for William until I came along. I know Katie gave him carrots and oats, but that must have been all! She didn't have time, so I don't blame her. But you should have seen William's stall! It took me over an hour the first time I cleaned it. Which wasn't until I was ready to groom him, because Katie was afraid to let me get too near him before that. The way it turned out, I didn't even have time to groom William that day. And there was no point in putting a clean horse in a dirty stall. So the stall got cleaned first.

I thought a lot about William and his problems. The trouble was, nobody rode him. A lot of people at Fox Run owned their own horse. The rest paid by the hour to ride a stable horse. Most of those weren't good riders, so they couldn't be trusted on a horse like William. That left William alone day in and day out, with no exercise, which meant that he got wilder and wilder. And the grooms only paid attention to the horses that were earning their keep.

Katie said a horse should be groomed and exercised every day. She said some of the girls who rode at Fox Run were rich and spoiled and didn't take care of their horses. She said they would put their horse back in the stall, all hot and sweaty, for somebody else to wash down and groom. If I owned a horse, I'd never do that!

When I finally got to groom William, Katie warned me to speak quietly and not make any sudden moves.

She patted William and said, "William, you remember Panky."

Then she stood very still and told me to stroke his neck and talk to him.

I said, "William, you remember me. I'm going to take care of you."

I think if William could have talked, he would have said, "Thank goodness!"

He was like a dirty old rug. I went over him with a curry comb, moving the comb in a circle. Then I brushed him, being real careful not to brush hard where the bones stick out. I knew that would hurt without anybody telling me. When I got through, his coat was soft and free of dust and lint.

He must have trusted me because he never did anything mean. After he got used to me, when he heard me coming down the aisle, he would stamp his foot, as if saying, "Hurry up!" And I came much more often. Every day when I could.

Once, I surprised him and slipped in quietly so he wouldn't recognize my footsteps or voice. William had his neck stretched out, like an alligator or something, and his ears were flat against his head, and he was trying to bite the horse in the next stall. When I spoke to him, his ears flicked forward and he looked straight ahead, as if he was showing me what a good boy he'd been! I had to laugh!

I always brought him an apple or a carrot. I never brought lumps of sugar because I thought it would hurt his teeth.

William liked to have me talk to him,

so I talked the whole time I groomed him. I'd say things like, "Well, hello, old boy. So you missed me! Well, you don't have to worry. I'm here now and I'm going to take care of you."

Sometimes, I would tell him my troubles, like if I'd had a bad day at school or Mother had been nagging me a lot or I had had to go to that silly psychiatrist again. He listened so quietly, you'd think he understood.

After about a month of this routine, William's coat felt like velvet. When I had to leave, I would bury my face in the soft fur of his neck and hug him.

"Be a good boy," I'd say. "I'll see you soon."

I hated to say goodbye.

William was such a lamb with me, I forgot how wild he was supposed to be. But one day, after I'd been actually grooming him for a couple of weeks, something happened to remind me. William was out in the aisle, so I could clean his stall, and Sandy, the exercise boy, walked by. Quick as a

flash, William's hind leg shot out. If Sandy hadn't jumped, he would have been badly kicked! I couldn't believe it! I tried to apologize.

"I'm sure he didn't mean that," I said. "He's usually so well behaved."

"Oh, sure!" said Sandy. "That's just his way of saying hello!"

"Well, he doesn't do it with me!" I said.

Katie had warned me never to come up on a horse from behind. She said you could scare a horse to death sneaking up on him. Sandy must have sneaked up on William!

"You have a calming effect on horses," Sandy called from down the aisle. He said it in a sarcastic way, but it was a compliment.

That made me proud! I wanted to think I was good with horses!

One thing I was sure of. Horses might not be smart, but they had their own way of knowing things. I guess you could call it intuition. They KNOW if somebody likes them. And since I'm crazy about horses, they just have to like me back! And I love William!

He'll always be my favorite horse in the world. I hope he lives as long as I do!

I was afraid of horses when I first started going home with Katie. They were so much bigger than me. I thought if one of them stepped on me by accident, it would really hurt!

After a while, I got used to how big they were. I was sure if I ever got a chance to get up on a horse, I wouldn't be afraid.

Chapter 11

I RUN AWAY

ONE DAY THERE was a morning visit to the psychiatrist when Mother talked for the whole hour with the door closed.

When we left, she was pretty quiet. After a while, she said, "I'm sorry about the little gift, Panky. That was a mistake. You see, I wanted to give you the things I liked. When I was your age, I loved pretty dresses. But times have changed, and so have little girls."

She smiled weakly.

"We'll just forget that yellow dress."

That was a relief! Maybe that doctor wasn't so bad after all!

"How about a cute jogging suit?" said Mother. "One with a drawstring at the waist? We could pull it tighter as you lose weight."

I gave up! Mother was never going to

ask me what I wanted! I hoped she wasn't thinking of sending me for more tennis lessons. She had never pushed them after that first time.

"Or maybe you'd like designer jeans. Mrs. Mahoney says they are very popular."

She was right there. Maybe it's because of the television ads. The girls in my class were crazy about designer jeans, and they didn't care how much they cost. One girl I knew said all she wanted for Christmas was designer jeans and bubble gum!

I didn't care about them, the reason being that I wouldn't look good in anything! You know the ads. Ever see anybody wearing designer jeans who was even a little bit fat?

Mother must have noticed I wasn't answering.

"We'll discuss this later," she said. "I don't want you to feel trapped. When you come home from school, we'll talk. Maybe we can agree on something."

That was funny, because trapped is what I felt! I had been trapped all fall.

Mother dropped me off at school in

time for lunch. I was glad because I wanted to ask Katie about William.

The news was not good. Katie told me as soon as we sat down.

"He's in serious trouble," she said. "If only he knew HOW serious!"

I forgot to be hungry.

Katie explained.

"He bucked off Sandy yesterday, and Sandy sprained his wrist. William pranced around as if he wished it were Sandy's neck. It was the first time William's been out of his stall, except when you groomed him, for over a week. With this cold weather, he was ready to explode! But the trouble is"—Katie's eyes widened—"he may have to go!"

I should have known things were going to get worse. William wasn't the kind of horse to be ignored! I had done a good job of grooming him, but I couldn't exercise him! This was terrible! Leaving Fox Run could only mean one thing. William was going to be sent to a dog food factory!

"Oh, no!" I gasped. "We mustn't let them send William away! He isn't mean or vicious! He thinks the whole world is against him!"

I felt a great longing to see William and comfort him.

"Oh, Katie!" I said. "Please let me take him his oats tonight! I can't come over after school, and I have to see him."

Katie didn't approve, but I wore her down.

"All right," she said, finally. "But don't blame me if you get caught! The oats are in the bin on the right, just as you come in."

I promised to be careful. It was worth the risk. At least William would know I cared!

After school, Mother and I talked, but we didn't come to any agreement, at least not anything I agreed to. So I might as well have been with William. That night, I lay quietly in bed until Mother and Daddy were asleep. Then, I got dressed, grabbed a flashlight, and made my way to Fox Run. There was a big moon out, and the air was icy cold. I wondered if the water in William's pail was frozen. It was an eerie feeling to be out alone late at night. It made me think of Halloween. But Halloween was long gone. Even Thanksgiving.

When I reached the stables, there was a night light burning, and I could see without a flashlight. I went straight to William's stall. He was not asleep. His head was hanging outside the gate as if he were waiting for me. He was swinging his head impatiently from side to side. I forgot to be afraid. I threw my arms around his neck.

"Oh, William!" I said. "Don't despair. I love you!"

William nuzzled my ear and blew his lips in a friendly, blubbering way. His tangled mane was soft against my face. When I went to get his oats, he whinnied and took to swinging his head again, as if he missed me. I fed him the oats from my hands, holding my hands out flat. I wasn't one bit afraid. Afterwards, I walked right in his stall and stroked his side.

It was warm in the stall, and I suddenly realized how tired I was. I had walked a long way, and now I was sleepy. But I didn't want to leave William. I lay down in the straw for a short rest, and before I knew it I was sound asleep.

When I woke up, it was morning. I was lying down, and William was lying down beside me. I had one arm flung over his shoulder. William was lying still, as if he didn't want to disturb me, but his eyes were open and staring. And no wonder! We were not alone. There, looking over the gate were Mother and Daddy and Hugo!

Daddy rushed over and scooped me up in his arms. Mother leaned against the gate, and I could tell she had been crying.

Later, I found out my parents had called the police, the school, and all the neighbors. The whole town had been out looking for me. Hugo was the one who stumbled on me, lying asleep in William's stall.

Now that they had found me, no one knew what to say. Then Hugo spoke up.

"We seem to have a future horsewoman here," he said briskly. "We'll have to put her to work."

He arranged with Mother for me to

have a trial lesson. Mother said if I liked it, she would sign up for more lessons.

I hadn't forgotten the arguments.

"Are you sure it won't cost too much?" I said, looking at Daddy.

Daddy smiled bravely.

"That's what parents are for," he said. "I'm glad to have a little girl to take care of."

Chapter 12

CONCLUSION

IT'S APRIL NOW, and I've been taking riding lessons for almost five months. I can hardly believe how unhappy I was at the beginning of school. Two things happened yesterday to show me how different things are.

First, when I got on the bus in the morning, Tiffany waved me to come over. She was saving the seat next to her for me! I sat down, not quite believing what was happening.

"I don't like Jennifer anymore," she said. "Do you?"

"She's OK," I said, cautiously.

"You know what makes me mad about Jennifer?" she said. "Everything I get, she has to buy one just like it. She got Nike sneakers as soon as she saw mine, and she bought a rain poncho like mine, too! It was the same color and everything!"

I could see where that might get on your nerves.

"It doesn't matter," she said. "We don't have much in common anymore. I'm really crazy about horses. I've ridden a couple of summers at camp so I'm not a beginner."

That might explain why she'd been unfriendly when I'd seen her at Fox Run. She felt above me. She must have changed her mind.

"Jennifer's into ballet," she said, "so we probably won't see much of each other anymore."

She suddenly noticed the way I was dressed.

"Hey! Those are neat riding pants! Where did you get them?"

I almost laughed out loud! Imagine Tiffany wanting to copy me! Jennifer got on at the next stop. She looked at us sort of funny, without speaking. Well, what the heck! She and Tiffany will probably be best friends again next week! But I have to admit, it felt good to have somebody save a seat for me, no matter what the reason!

The second good thing that happened was in the cafeteria.

Katie was dressed in riding clothes too, because Mother is taking me to Fox Run right after school for a lesson and sometimes now Katie takes a lesson when I do. We were both wearing a green neckband and a green ribbon in our hair. Katie's hair is longer and a ribbon looked better on her ponytail. The biggest difference in the way we looked was that Katie wore boots and I had on regular shoes.

I didn't care if Katie looked better than I did. I felt good wearing my riding clothes to school. I remember when I used to see kids at school with their tennis rackets or hockey sticks and I thought they were showing off. Maybe they were, in a way. Maybe I am, too. I hope when people see me they think, "That's the REAL Panky!"

Because as far as I'm concerned, this is the real me!

Well, what happened was this:

Joey Watson walked by and he did this big double-take, staring and blinking as if he couldn't believe his eyes. I couldn't help it. My heart just sank! I thought, "Oh, no! Not again!"

Then Joey gave this big neigh and started running around Katie and me in circles, like he was galloping.

Katie laughed, and I did too.

"He's just trying to impress us," Katie whispered.

He was, too!

I guess Joey's all right.

These aren't big things, but they made me feel very, very good!

I'm a lot happier than I used to be, but I haven't turned into an angel overnight. I found out this morning that I can still blow up at Mother.

Today's Saturday, so I came down to breakfast late and Mother said, "Guess what? Tiffany Calder's mother called to invite you to Tiffany's birthday party. Isn't that nice?"

I wasn't exactly surprised since all Tif-

fany's been talking about for a week is her birthday party. Practically every girl in class is invited but Katie, and Katie feels awful!

"I'm not going," I said.

"Not going?" said Mother. "Why not?"

She didn't remind me that this was the first birthday party I've been invited to since moving here.

"I thought it was so nice that you were making friends," she said.

I didn't like the way that sounded. In case Mother hadn't noticed, I DO have a friend!

I stomped out of the kitchen without answering. Daddy followed me out.

"What was all that about?" he asked. "I thought you liked birthday parties."

"Tiffany isn't inviting Katie," I said. "She's my best friend, and her feelings are really hurt!"

"Well, why didn't you say that?" said Daddy. "Now, you go right back in the kitchen and explain. Talk about hurt feelings! How do you think Mother feels when you stomp out of the room?"

To tell you the truth, I wasn't too proud of myself. I guess sometimes I blame Mother for things that are not her fault.

Daddy hadn't finished.

"Panky, has it ever occurred to you that Mother may get lonely? She's having to get used to a new place, too."

I think I'd known that right along.

"Why can't you two be friends?" said Daddy. "You could start out by saying what you think."

Daddy looked tired. I noticed his wrinkles have sort of grown into his face. They didn't make him look mean. He looked like a grizzled old St. Bernard, pleading with me to be nice.

"We've got to find some way," he said, "of being a little kinder to the people we love."

I was sorry I'd acted the way I had. Daddy was right. I had to be nicer to Mother.

I ran back to the kitchen. I didn't apologize, but I did explain about Katie being left out and that I had to stick up for my best friend.

To my surprise, Mother was very understanding.

"I can promise you this," she said. "When you have YOUR birthday party, Katie will be the first person to get invited!"

That made me feel better. Maybe I would go to Tiffany's party after all. I'd heard she was going to have a magician. Anyway, as long as Katie knew she was still my best friend, she wouldn't feel too bad.

After that, things settled into their usual Saturday routine. Mother was sorting through my old clothes, trying to decide what to give to the Thrift Shop. There was a lot to get rid of because I've lost so much weight.

Mother called me in to show me something. She had propped up my first riding pants so they looked as if they were going to walk off by themselves. Boy! were they gross! I couldn't imagine who would want them unless there was a fat midget somewhere looking for pants to wear riding her fat midget elephant!

"They're positively HUMONGOUS!" I said.

We laughed.

Daddy heard us and smiled when I came downstairs.

"We don't need a psychiatrist around here anymore," he said. "This family's getting along pretty well."

That night, Mother cooked a wonderful dinner. We all eat together now, when we're home, and we eat the same food. None of it's fattening, and it's delicious! Mother bought a diet cookbook with really neat recipes. She even baked low calorie brownies for dessert.

The only thing is, she still has this nervous way of watching me eat. I suppose it will take a long time for her to get over that.

"I guess the best way to diet is to forget it," I said, irritably.

Daddy cleared his throat, and I got the message.

"Thanks for your help, Mother," I said. "It's easy to diet with meals like this!"

Mother beamed.

She said, "Panky, we haven't discussed your reward. You've lost a lot of weight, and you really deserve something. What would you like?

This was the first time Mother had ever asked me what I wanted. I might never have the chance again.

"BOOTS!" I shouted.

Mother and Daddy laughed; I did too. I was really happy! Boots were all I needed to make me feel like a real horsewoman! Later, when I went up to bed, Mother offered me another brownie, to show there were no hard feelings, I guess. I took it, but I wasn't hungry.

I was almost asleep when Daddy came in to say goodnight. I had the feeling he wanted to talk. He has that look a lot of the time now, as if he's trying to say something.

When I was little, Daddy used to read me fairy tales at bedtime. We haven't talked much since then. I wondered if he remembered. I closed my eyes and pretended to be asleep.

Daddy brushed a brownie crumb from the corner of my mouth and kissed me on the cheek. I couldn't help smiling.

"Good night, Panky-Poo," he whispered. "I'm glad about William."

So am I, Daddy! So am I! William is great! He's the best animal I've ever known and I love him, even if he isn't mine.

It's hard to believe that only six or seven months ago, I was fat and had no friends. Now I have a wonderful best friend, Katie, and a terrific hobby. I know who I am now. I'm a horsewoman and I always will be! And the best thing about learning to ride is that there's so much to learn, there's no end to it. I'm just getting started!

About the Author

Nancy Saxon grew up in a small southern town, then went to Salem College in Winston-Salem, North Carolina, and Barnard College in New York City. She met her husband, Charles Saxon, when he was training to be a pilot in her home town. They have three children.

Together they make a family of animal lovers, and like Panky, Nancy Saxon thinks it would be great to have a house full of animals. Instead, they have settled on one devoted Irish water spaniel, Bessie.

About the Illustrator

Charles Saxon has been a staff cartoonist for *The New Yorker* for twenty-seven years. He grew up in Brooklyn, thought he wanted to be a doctor, but discovered at Columbia University that he preferred art. He has published two collections of cartoons: *Oh, Happy, Happy, Happy!* and *One Man's Fancy*.